What's Yours is Mine

and other short stories

Stefania Hartley

THE*SICILIAN*MAMA

To Mamma and Papà x

CONTENTS

1 What's Yours is Mine   1

2 Better to Have Loved   14

3 Charity Begins at Home   41

4 The Sleep Doctor   54

5 Tanino's Chair   66

   Other books   79

   About the Author   84

1. WHAT'S YOURS IS MINE

Tanino was enjoying a bean soup when the doorbell rang. Melina sprang up from the table, scuttled down the corridor and answered the door.

"Hello, Rosanna, my love," Tanino heard her say. It was their daughter, who lived in the flat below.

"Hello, Mum. I need to borrow a screwdriver from Dad."

Tanino groaned. He would have to get up and fetch the screwdriver out of his toolbox, right in the middle of his meal. Also, if Rosanna needed a screwdriver, she probably had to fix something and needed his help.

He dropped his spoon in his bowl

and started heaving himself up from his chair, when he heard Melina say, "I'll go and get it for you."

Surely she didn't even know where he kept his toolbox. But Tanino was curious to see how long it would take her to come and ask him, so he sat down again.

A few seconds later, he heard a clanging of metal and then Melina's voice.

"Here you go, darling."

"I don't need the whole toolbox, Mum. I only need one screwdriver."

Goodness gracious! Melina had found his toolbox and was giving away the whole thing! Surely she'd come and ask him first. Again, he was curious to see how far Melina would go before she thought of consulting him, so he fought the impulse to run to the door and reclaim his most treasured possession.

He heard the tinkling of small metal items, then Rosanna's voice. "Here, this one should be the right size."

"Is something broken? Do you need your father to come down to fix it?"

Now Melina was even offering his services without asking him.

"No, thanks. Michele can do it. He wouldn't like Dad to step on his toes."

Trust Melina to get him on the wrong side of his son-in-law!

"I'll bring the screwdriver back as soon as we've finished," Rosanna said.

"No need. Keep it, darling."

Tanino's eyes almost popped out of his skull. His wife was giving his stuff away!

"Thanks, Mum," Rosanna said.

He should be the one to be thanked!

As soon as Melina returned to the table, Tanino harrumphed.

"That was Rosanna," she said.

"I know. And you've given her my screwdriver without asking me."

"Did you need it?" she asked, looking genuinely surprised.

"That's not the point: you can't give away stuff that's not yours."

"We've always said that what's mine is yours and what's yours is mine."

"Except my toolbox. Didn't you see my initials carved on the lid?"

"So what? My initials are carved on your wedding ring but that doesn't make it mine."

Tanino didn't know what to say. Melina swallowed the last mouthful of her lunch, got up and began to clear the table. Tanino was still a little stunned so he wasn't in time to grab a hunk of bread before she cleared away the bread basket.

***

Melina couldn't help it. If anyone asked her for anything, she would give it to them. She'd take the food out of her mouth if someone asked for it. And, as she viewed Tanino like an extension of herself, she would take food out of his mouth too. She knew that it wasn't right, but she just couldn't help herself.

And now she was so sorry to have given away Tanino's screwdriver that she went to the hardware store to buy him a replacement.

"Signora, you're the second person to ask for a screwdriver in the last half hour. Which type and size would you like?"

Up until that moment, Melina had thought that all screwdrivers were more or less the same.

"Which one do you recommend?"

The man snorted with laughter.

"Signora, it's not up to me. It depends on what you need it for."

"I don't know: it's not for me, of course," she said, a little offended. "If you're not going to help me choose, I'll have the same as the one you've just sold."

"I'm not sure that I have another one."

The threat of a shortage only made Melina keener.

"I want that one and no other."

The man rolled his eyes and plodded to the back of the shop.

"You're lucky: two millimetres slotted, the last one."

Melina felt very satisfied. Such a sought-after screwdriver must be better than Tanino's old one.

On the way home she also bought the ingredients to make *arancine*. Cooking one of Tanino's favourite dishes would complete her atonement.

When she got home, he was out. She immediately put the rice on the hob and the mince in a pan to make the sauce for the filling. Then she rolled the rice around the meat filling and coated the balls in breadcrumbs before deep-frying them in batches.

Arancine were as much work as risotto, Bolognese sauce and French fries all wrapped in one, and that was why she rarely cooked them.

She was frying the last batch when the doorbell rang.

"Dad sent me to give you this back. He has just bought himself one," her grandchild told her, handing her back

Tanino's screwdriver.

"Thank you, darling. I'm cooking *arancine*. Would you like one?"

"Yes!" Valentina exclaimed with sparkly eyes.

Grandma and granddaughter then went to the kitchen, where Melina chose an *arancina* that was warm but not too hot and gave it to Valentina.

"It's delicious!" the child said, munching away.

Melina's heart leapt with happiness and she put six more on a plate.

"Take these home. You won't ruin your appetite if you have two each as a starter. So long as you promise that you'll still eat whatever meal your mum has prepared."

"Mum is still at work. Dad is cooking."

Melina added more *arancine* to the plate. In such an emergency…

"Thank you, Grandma," Valentina said with a huge smile.

"Melina, what you're doing isn't fair,"

Giovanna, her next-door neighbour, called from the door of Melina's flat.

"What have I done?" Melina replied.

"You fry *arancine* with the door open and now the entire building smells delicious. What are we going to do when our husbands come home and find that the smell isn't coming from their flats? They'll be very disappointed."

"Oh no, we don't want disappointed husbands!" Melina made another plate of *arancine* and thrust it into her neighbour's hands. "Here, my dear, take these home."

Giovanna made a little show of refusing—but without putting the plate down. Melina insisted and Giovanna quickly accepted.

It was only when Melina was alone again that she suddenly remembered the batch still sizzling in the pan. She rushed to the kitchen but it was too late: the last *arancine* had been fiercely browned.

Melina pulled them out of the oil and put them aside. This batch would have to be for her.

She had just finished laying the table when the doorbell rang again. It was Valentina with an empty plate almost as big as a serving dish.

"Dad says if you have a couple more *arancine* we'll make it a meal and he won't have to cook."

"Sure!"

Melina filled Valentina's plate without leaving any empty space.

"Wow, thank you so much, Grandma!" Valentina popped an *arancina* in her mouth—which Melina instantly replaced—and left.

Melina looked at the table. The only *arancine* left were the burnt ones. She imagined Giovanna serving her husband a plateful of perfectly cooked *arancine* while Tanino crunched on charcoal balls.

And there wasn't even enough for her!

She sat down and put her head in her hands. Then the lock of the front door clanged. Tanino was home.

"I came up in the lift with our neighbour and I bet him that the smell was coming from my flat. He said no, it must be from his flat. And I won," Tanino called from the hall. "It's *arancine*, isn't it? Yummy!"

"I'm not feeling very well. I'm going to bed," Melina said and retreated to her room.

***

Tanino only agreed to sit down to lunch without Melina after she profusely assured him that she wasn't unwell and only needed a little feet-up time.

Arancine, on the other hand, were just what he needed. He had been to the hardware store to replace the screwdriver and had found that the size he needed was sold out.

The *arancine* would cheer him up. He lifted the fly-cover. Ah, just as dark as he liked them! They didn't make them that dark in the shops because some people would say that they were burnt.

As he bit into one, the extra-crispy skin shattered and an explosion of taste burst into his mouth. Oh, how he loved his wife when she cooked for him!

Hold on. She hadn't put aside any for herself! Tanino would have happily scoffed the entire plateful but, instead, he only ate half. He had just got up to take the remaining *arancine* to the bedroom for Melina when she appeared on the threshold.

Her eyes darted to the plate of *arancine* that Tanino was holding.

"There's no need to throw them in the bin. I'll eat them if you don't like them," she said.

"Bin? Why would I ever put your delicious *arancine* in the bin? I was bringing them to you, dear."

A big smile lit up Melina's face. "Did you like them?"

"Very much! Now come and sit down."

He put an arm around her shoulders and steered her towards her seat, then put the plate in front of her.

"You can't give them to me: they are yours," she said.

Tanino smiled. "Didn't we say that what's mine is yours?"

Melina's cheeks reddened. "Wait a moment." She got up and left the room. She came back clutching her handbag. "This is your screwdriver, which Michele has returned, and this is a new one I bought for you."

He took the two screwdrivers and hugged her.

"So you bought the last one at the hardware shop! The shopkeeper almost fainted when I asked for a two millimetres slotted head. He said that I was the third customer in a row asking for the same thing. The first one must have been Michele, and the second one was you! But how in the world did you know what type and size to buy?"

"I asked for the same as his last customer's. I thought it must be the most popular one."

Tanino smiled and shook his head in disbelief. He put his old screwdriver in his pocket. Then he pulled a marker pen out of a drawer and started scribbling on the new screwdriver.

"There's no need to write your name on it, Tanino. I won't give away your stuff anymore," Melina said, looking very contrite.

He looked over at her with a small smile. "I'm not writing my name on it, Melina. I'm writing yours."

2. BETTER TO HAVE LOVED

Pericle had been away from home for months doing the compulsory military training that all Italian men had to undertake as they reached adulthood.

The driver had picked him up at the train station and Pericle had insisted on driving himself. After a sleepless night on the train, the drive on the bumpy dirt track was tiring. When he turned a corner and saw his ancestral home, Villa Lingualarga, his strength came back. His mother was waiting for him at the top of the grand baroque staircase.

"You look thinner, Periclù," she said tenderly, holding his cheeks between her palms.

"I'm just the same as before, Mammà," he replied, surprised at being treated like a child after having been a man for many months.

"Come and have something to eat. Then rest, because tonight we have important visitors."

"Yes, Mammà, as you command!" he joked.

***

Salvatore was clipping the rosebush when Pinuccia appeared at kitchen door. He averted his gaze, embarrassed at being caught looking. She hurried with light, quick steps towards him.

"Good morning, Salvatore. Madam would like some strawberries for young sir, please."

The other maidservants were polite only to the bosses, but Pinuccia was polite to everyone. He nodded but couldn't get a word out of his throat, not even a "yes". It wasn't just shyness: it only happened with Pinuccia, not with the other girls.

***

"Watch out, Pinuccia. Salvatore doesn't only grow strawberries but cucumbers too!" Rosa cackled.

"You should wash your tongue with soap, Rosa," Caterina, the old cook, scolded.

The other maidservants in the kitchen giggled. Everyone knew why Pinuccia always volunteered to go and get the vegetables.

"Pinuccia," Caterina told her one evening when they were alone, "not many men will marry a girl without a dowry. Plus, you know that Don Girolamo doesn't allow marriage between his staff. What would Salvatore do without a job? Be careful."

"I'm not expecting anything. I'm just happy watching him work."

"But one day he'll bring in a wife from outside and then, how will you feel? Forget him, Pinù."

"I can't."

***

After his mother and father, the next person Pericle went to greet was Salvatore. They had played together since childhood and they had grown up like brothers and best friends.

"Master Pericle!" Salvatore cried when Pericle appeared at the vegetable patch.

"Don't call me 'Master'." That word, which Salvatore usually used only when other people were around, irritated Pericle. It was as if his absence from Villa Lingualarga had put a distance between them.

Salvatore dropped the hoe and hugged him.

"How was the army?" Salvatore asked, with a hint of shame.

The only son of a widow, he was exempt from the national service, but he felt as if he was a deserter.

"So-so. Tell me about here instead. How have things been without me?"

"Your mum has counted the days. I've had to make sure that, today, I had enough flowers for all the rooms. I didn't know you liked flowers so much."

"They're not for me: we have visitors tonight."

"That explains why the kitchen is asking for so many things today."

"Or maybe someone in the kitchen just wants to see you often!"

Pericle meant it just as banter and was surprised to see Salvatore blush. "Gosh, you like one of the girls from the kitchen, don't you?" he asked with the bluntness of an old friend.

Salvatore blushed even more. "I like Pinuccia."

"You know my dad doesn't allow it, don't you?"

"I do. But I wondered…Do you think you could talk to your father, ask him if he'll let me marry her?"

Pericle was stunned. His friend—twenty-one years old like him—was already thinking of marriage.

"Will you ask, please?" Salvatore's eyes burned with the desire to make

Pinuccia his wife.

"I will. But what will you do if he says no?"

"I'll look for another job."

"What about your mother?"

"I'll find somebody who'll take us all: Mum, Pinuccia, and me. Please, ask your father."

"Shouldn't you ask Pinuccia first?"

"I don't want to until I know what I can offer her. Will you speak to your father, please?"

"I will. I promise."

***

Don Girolamo glanced at his son when he entered the study. The desk lamp drizzled a stingy light on the green leather desk and the old man bent over large files thick with numbers. "What is it?"

"If you're busy, I'll come back later," Pericle said.

"If it's not urgent, come back tomorrow after the visitors have gone."

How come everyone cared so much

about these visitors? "Who's coming tonight?"

"The Count and the Countess of Altamo." Don Girolamo sounded irritated.

Pericle realised it wasn't a good time to ask more questions and left.

When the visitors' car arrived Pericle was surprised to see a third person, whom his father hadn't mentioned. The count and the countess, too, seemed to pay little attention to her. Was she a lady-in-waiting?

"Ah, this is our daughter, Laura." The count introduced the girl distractedly.

Laura stepped forward and smiled graciously, as if she was used to being forgotten. Pericle immediately felt sympathy for her.

At the dinner table, Don Girolamo and the count began a conversation about a new property tax, while their wives found a common interest in cultivated pearls.

"How was your journey?" Pericle

asked Laura, from duty to entertain her.

"Pleasant." She seemed surprised to be spoken to. "Papà drives very well."

That was a topic that ignited Pericle's interest.

"Do you drive too?"

She looked at him with surprise. Clearly nobody had asked her that question before.

"No, I don't. But I would love to learn."

"I love driving. If your father doesn't want to teach you, I will."

Pericle was surprised by the ease with which he spoke to her. It felt like they were old friends.

She glanced at her father, still busy talking. "Papà will never teach me. He hasn't even allowed me to study." The smile disappeared from her face.

"Is he very traditional?"

"No. It's because I suffer from poor health and he's overprotective."

Was this why the count had almost forgotten to introduce her and why Don

Girolamo hadn't mentioned her, either? Perhaps the count hadn't told him.

Laura changed the topic. "Tell me about yourself. What else do you like, apart from driving?"

"I love playing the piano."

They talked about music, books and their favourite painters. The more they talked, the more Pericle felt attracted to her warmth, her sensitivity and the depth of her thoughts.

***

The next morning, as he watched the count's car roaring down the windy drive, Pericle noticed Salvatore working in the lemon grove and suddenly remembered his promise.

"Papà, I have something to ask you."

Don Girolamo's brow furrowed. The count's visit seemed to have depressed him, so maybe it wasn't a good time to ask.

"What is it?"

"It's about Salvatore. He would like to get married."

"To whom?"

"Pinuccia, from the kitchen. I know the rule against marrying within our staff, but Salvatore was born here. He didn't choose to work here."

"Rules are for everyone. If he wants to continue to work here, he must find a wife somewhere else. If he wants to marry Pinuccia, he'll have to leave."

"But I don't want to lose him, Dad. You yourself said that he's an excellent gardener."

"If he's more attached to Pinuccia than to you, it's his choice. But if he decides to stay, tell him he'd better stop looking at girls if he wants to keep his job. I don't want any funny business going on." Don Girolamo moved on to talk about the model and make of the count's car and Pericle understood that their conversation on Salvatore's future was over.

Salvatore took the news much better than Pericle had expected.

"I'm sorry. I hoped Dad would make

an exception."

"It's OK. At least now I know how things stand and what I need to do."

"What will you do?"

"I'll propose to Pinuccia and, if she agrees to marry me, I'll look for a job."

"You've always lived here. Your father worked here. How will you do it?" Salvatore had never ventured further than the village.

"Where there's a will, there's a way."

Pericle thought that there was more bravery in his friend than in many of the officers he'd met in the army. He almost hoped Pinuccia would reject him so that he'd stay, but was ashamed of his selfishness and chased the thought away.

***

Pinuccia took a basket from the kitchen and went looking for Salvatore.

"Good morning. May I have some carrots and a bunch of lettuce for lunch?" she said shyly.

"You always ask me for things. Today

24

I'll ask you for something," he said.

"Have I done something wrong?" she said, alarmed.

"Yes: you have stolen my heart." He smiled.

"Pardon?" Pinuccia was sure she had misheard. This was so unlike Salvatore.

"If you're not going to return my heart to me, then, please, marry me. I love you, Pinù."

He fell on his knees and Pinuccia gasped and dropped her basket.

"I know that if we marry we'll lose our jobs, but I'll look for another job and, when I've found it, I'll take you with me. Your love means everything to me!"

He took her hand and his eyes shone with hope. He had just spoken to her more words than he had ever done in her seventeen years of life. Was this the same Salvatore that she sometimes caught glancing shyly at her from the end of the garden? The man who never looked at her straight in the eyes? What an effort this proposal must have cost him!

Thoughts and feelings whirred inside her. She wanted to shout, "Yes!" but her lips couldn't move.

"What do you say, Pinù? Have I offended you?"

Finally, her lips obeyed. "Yes, Salvatò, I want to marry you more than anything. I don't care if we have to leave here. I want to be with you forever, wherever you are."

***

The count and his wife reciprocated the Lingualarga dinner with an invitation to their mansion.

Pericle felt excited at the idea of seeing Laura again, even if he couldn't work out why. She wasn't a striking beauty, but she had something about her that attracted him as no other girl had.

Altamo House was grander than Villa Lingualarga but it, too, bore the signs of age and lack of repairs.

The count's son, Antonio, who worked as a lawyer and lived in Palermo, was at the dinner. Pericle sensed that he had been summoned by his father specially to meet him.

Antonio asked him about his plans for the future and seemed shocked to learn that Pericle didn't have any.

"I guess I'll manage the estate, helping Papà."

"I strongly advise you against it. There's no money in cultivating the land now. Times have changed. I've seen many titled gentlemen end up in dingy little flats in Palermo because they could no longer afford to keep their ancestral homes. Many of them are my clients and are spending great amounts of money and time fighting off creditors instead of getting a job. Nobody, not even a prince, can afford to say that they are too posh to work, these days. There are many titled people in law offices in Palermo, in architects' and engineers' studies. Those who have any capital left invest it into a business and become entrepreneurs."

Pericle went to bed with his head pounding with worry about his future and his heart saddened by not having been able to exchange anything more than a couple of greetings with Laura.

The next morning, while he was in the stables packing the car for the drive home, he saw Laura approaching. She wasn't wearing riding gear, so she must be coming to see him.

"Don't forget you promised you would teach me how to drive. Our parents are discussing politics at the breakfast table, so you won't be leaving anytime soon," she said with a cheeky smile.

Pericle was more than happy to oblige. They jumped in the car and drove all around the estate, through woods and fields, whooping and laughing.

"It's a shame your father didn't let you study. You learn very quickly."

"According to him, I should be thankful I'm still alive. I've got bad lungs and have been close to death on many occasions. Since the doctors told him that I wouldn't live past twenty, my father has acted as if I was already dead. But I'm twenty-one now," she said proudly.

"Maybe he's trying to protect himself. He must have suffered a lot and he doesn't want to suffer more."

"A life lived trying to protect yourself is not worth living, if you ask me. I'd much rather live like I do than like he does."

"How do you live?"

"Loving. Loving all the way, until I die."

As she said these words her eyes sparkled and she looked at him intensely.

When they returned to the stables, their parents were waiting for them and the magic was over.

That day, in the silence of his car

journey home with his parents, Pericle admitted to himself that he was in love.

As soon as he got home he wrote a letter to Laura, and it became the first of many between them, in which they shared their innermost thoughts and feelings, including their reciprocal affection.

Seeing each other, though, was now out of the question, as Laura had moved with her family to their summer residence, an eight-hour drive away, and the invitations to dinner had been suspended.

But if Laura became his fiancée, Pericle would be able to go and visit her. He felt ready to propose, and he was confident that the count would not oppose their engagement.

But the way his own father had crushed Salvatore's hopes of marrying Pinuccia didn't bode well, and Pericle feared the worst.

He was waiting for a favourable time to broach the subject, when his father called him into his study.

"Now that you're back from the army and you've had a little rest, it's time to think about your future," Don Girolamo said.

"Yes, Papà. I wanted to talk to you about it too."

His father continued as if he hadn't heard him.

"This estate is not profitable anymore, and agriculture is struggling everywhere. Times have changed and landowners—aristocratic or not—are taking other employment. There's no shame if somebody like you decides to work, like Count Altamo's son. You must enrol into the university in Palermo and enter one of the honourable professions, like him."

This was not what Pericle had expected.

"How many years will I have to study?"

"Four, I think. Then you'll land a job in Palermo with Antonio's help."

By the time Pericle got a job and could marry Laura, she would be at least twenty-five! It wouldn't be fair to ask her to wait that long. But Pericle had never opposed his father's will. "Father, what about marriage? I'd like to get married sooner than that."

"Really? Have you got a girl in mind?" Don Girolamo looked genuinely surprised that his son was thinking about such matters.

"Laura Altamo."

"Oh. But the girl is sickly. You know, don't you?"

"What of it? I want her to be my wife. Father, please, let me marry her. She could come and live in Palermo with me while I study. Maybe we could share her brother's flat, if he doesn't mind. She might want to study too. We could go to university together. I could try to find work helping Antonio, even before I graduate. I'll do anything, Papà. Please, let me marry her," Pericle pleaded.

"You don't know what you're saying.

It's utter nonsense! This is what love does: it turns sensible men into lunatics. Look at you and Salvatore."

Pericle rushed out of the room in a mixture of despair, embarrassment and anger. Why was his father so hard, so lacking in understanding?

For the following days, Pericle played the piano from morning till evening, one heart-rending song after another. This was the only balm for his crushed heart.

"Periclù, this music is making everyone sad. Are you unhappy?" his mother asked him one day.

Pericle told her about Laura, about his father's plans for him, and his desire to marry her before she was promised to someone else.

"Her health, Periclù... do you realise that she might not be able to bear you any children?"

"I know, Mamma, but I still want to marry her. We have written to each other many letters and I know that we will be very happy together."

"A happy marriage is a blessing that neither money, titles nor beauty—nor even health—can give. If you are sure about her, I will talk to you father."

She led him to her bedroom where she took a beautiful diamond ring out of her jewellery box.

"You need an engagement ring, Periclù. Take this. It was your grandma's. She had a very happy marriage."

"Shouldn't we wait to hear what Papà says?"

"Don't worry. He never denies me anything I ask him. But I never ask him anything that he'll have to deny me.

***

Just as his mother had promised, his father agreed to the wedding, under the condition that Pericle completed his studies afterwards.

As soon as the news was delivered to him, Pericle got into the car and in five hours and seven minutes was at the count's summer house.

He rushed up the stairs and knocked on the door. Laura opened it.

At first, she didn't seem to recognise him, but as soon as she did, a look of pure joy ignited her face.

Pericle went down on one knee, told her all that she meant to him, and asked her to marry him.

"Yes," she answered, radiant like the August sunshine.

The count reacted to Pericle's request of his daughter's hand with the usual indifference. But, after dinner, he invited Pericle into his study with the excuse of a smoke.

"Are you aware of Laura's health situation?" he asked as soon as the two of them were alone.

"Yes, but I still want to marry her."

"Loving Laura means suffering." The count's voice quivered.

"I prefer to love and suffer than not to love," Pericle said seriously.

"Very well. It's your choice."

The count moved on to practical matters regarding their future, like their accommodation in Palermo, which he would ask Antonio to arrange while Pericle studied for his degree.

The date for the wedding was set for September and the reception would be held at Villa Lingualarga.

Pericle spent a few blissful days at the count's home, playing the piano and singing with Laura, taking walks with her through the gardens, going for car rides and just enjoying each other's company.

When he returned to Villa Lingualarga, his heart was brimming with so much happiness that it felt like it would burst if he didn't share it, so he rushed to Salvatore's workshop to tell him his news.

"Salvo, I've got news to tell you!"

Salvatore turned a strained face to him. His skin looked tight around his cheekbones and his eyes had bags under them.

"Are you OK, Salvo? Did Pinuccia say no?" Pericle asked, worried.

"No, quite the opposite, thank God! But I haven't found a job yet. I've looked as far as Sumeci, but nothing. My mother is worried that Don Girolamo will boot me out before I find one."

"I won't let him!"

***

Days went by, and Salvatore's hopes of finding a new job got weaker and weaker.

Pericle felt guilty about being happy while his friend was suffering, but his happiness didn't last long. A telegram from his father-in-law-to-be arrived one morning in early September.

Laura has pneumonia.

Pericle jumped into the car and raced to the count's summer house.

He burst through the front door and ran inside, calling out her name as he went.

He was directed to her bedroom by

the servants, and there he found her lying in bed, white as the sheet, with her mother sitting by her bedside. In her ghostly pallor, Laura looked already like an angel.

"Thanks be to God! She's been calling your name all through the night," the countess said.

Pericle sat down and held Laura's hand. She squeezed his weakly.

"You won't leave me so soon, will you, my love?" he begged, alarmed by the icy coldness of her skin.

"I want to stay, but I don't think I can. I'm sorry, Pericle. Thank you for loving me," she said with all the breath she could manage.

Pericle stayed by her side, holding her hand, kissing it, stroking and mopping her feverish brow, until she gently closed her eyes for the last time. And he cried.

***

The count cried bitter tears at his daughter's funeral, too, and people murmured that they were crocodile tears and that he'd never really cared about his daughter. But Pericle knew better.

A letter was found on Laura's writing desk, shakily written on the day her fever started. She thanked Pericle for making that last month the happiest in her life.

She asked that her dowry and wedding dress be given to a disadvantaged girl who was engaged to be married to a good honest man.

Pericle immediately suggested Pinuccia, and Laura's parents agreed. Then Pericle gathered his courage and went to talk to his father.

"Papà, Laura and I haven't been able to enjoy a life together or to give life to children. But our love can live on if we share it with others. I ask you, in memory of Laura, to let Salvatore and Pinuccia get married in our home and have the wedding party you had prepared for us."

Before his son's generosity, Don

Girolamo relented. He also allowed them to continue living and working in Villa Lingualarga, as a special exception in memory of his son's fiancé.

Salvatore and Pinuccia were overjoyed and thanked Pericle. "You will always be welcome in our home and, every night, we—and any children we'll have—will say a prayer for you."

3. CHARITY BEGINS AT HOME

After retiring, Tanino had become even more careful with money. That was not the case with his wife.

Perhaps it was because Melina hadn't retired—housewives were never allowed to retire, she often pointed out—or maybe it was because she had never had to endure a bad boss, unpleasant colleagues or the slavery of the clock.

Every Friday for the last fifty years, Tanino had given her a weekly allowance and her only job had been to spend it.

No wonder she slept like a baby every night: there were no money worries on her horizon. He, on the other hand, ended up doing the worrying for them both.

He sat down for his lunch. Pasta with beans again. The food of the poor. Surely they could afford a little meat or fish every now and then. Where did all the money he gave her go?

"Why don't we eat pasta with Bolognese *ragù* every now and then?" he asked Melina.

"Beef is expensive."

"But I give you fifty euros every week and I don't even eat very much."

"Today is Thursday and all there is left is one euro seventy," she said curtly.

"Where has all the money gone?" He opened his arms in a gesture of exasperated surrender. "I know where it's gone: to charity. To the church."

Tanino had nothing against the many charities Melina supported, or the beggar who smiled sweetly at Melina every time she went in and out of the church. He was even a good friend of their parish priest. But the mouthwatering smells that wafted out of the presbytery around mealtimes sometimes made him wish he had been called to holy orders.

Melina heaved a sigh and rolled her eyes. At least she wasn't trying to deny that she gave away a lot of their money to charity.

"Charity starts at home," Tanino pressed on. "When Jesus said, 'I want mercy, not sacrifice', he meant that he'd rather you had mercy on your husband than give alms."

"No, he didn't."

"Then how about 'love your neighbour as yourself'? Who is a closer neighbour than the person who sleeps right beside you at night? The person who is tied up to you for better and for worse, for richer and for—Heaven forbid—poorer?"

"Ah, is that how you feel, Tanino? 'Tied up' to me?"

"Darling, it was just a figure of speech!"

Melina scraped her chair back and stormed out of the room, leaving her husband to eat his lunch alone. Like a priest.

***

Melina had overreacted to Tanino's comments because she knew that she was in the wrong, and "in the wrong" was a place she hated as much as the dentist's.

That week she had given away to charity almost half her weekly shopping money and next week she would probably do the same. Each time the mass's offertory basket glided before her, or a beggar's hand stretched out to her, she could not help giving some money.

That was even if she had already donated to the church by monthly contribution, and if the beggar had already received plenty of coins from her on the way in.

She usually managed to make do until the end of the week by cooking with cheap seasonal greens and pulses, but this month she had a problem. She needed to save some money for a purchase that Tanino must not know about or he might oppose it. For the first time in her life, Melina had money worries.

**

Tanino decided that enough was enough. For the next couple of weeks, he would give Melina only half her usual shopping allowance. It would be sufficient to buy the bread, beans and pasta—the cheap stuff she was bent on feeding him.

With the money saved, he would buy a nice gift for his mother hundredth's birthday. She had always appreciated the bag of lemon-flavoured boiled sweets he gave her on every birthday, but perhaps all that sugar wasn't too good for her now that she was getting on a bit. And it probably wasn't a big enough gift for reaching one hundred.

No, he would buy her some perfume

this time. He had seen just the thing in the *profumeria* downstairs.

"Twenty-five euros for our weekly shopping is too little!" Melina protested when he broke the news to her.

"Give it a go. If it isn't enough, bring me all the receipts and we'll review your budget. I need to save money this month, Melina."

"What for?"

"A private matter."

Over the years they'd had plenty of arguments about his alleged stinginess when buying gifts and he wasn't going to open that can of worms.

Melina narrowed her eyes and pursed her lips, then she went into the hall, slipped on her coat and grabbed her bag.

"Where are you going?"

She snorted. "It's a private matter," she said, and left.

***

"This shape is out of fashion. The most I can give you for a ring like this is twenty euros," the pawn-shop man told her.

"Twenty euros? No thanks!"

Melina snatched back her ring and marched to the door. But she hadn't yet left when she stopped. The man's offer wasn't a bluff, because he'd made no attempt to call her back.

Where else would she get the money for her mother-in-law's hundredth-birthday present? Even if, that week, she didn't give a single cent to any church or beggar, it would be impossible to squirrel anything away from the revised shopping allowance without starving herself and Tanino.

She certainly wasn't going to ask Tanino to buy a better present than the usual packet of sweets for his mother. If Tanino couldn't be made to buy her a better present, Melina would. She turned around. Twenty euros wasn't enough for the perfume she had set her heart on, but perhaps she might get a little discount, given that she lived in the same building as the shop.

Melina humbly returned to the hatch and slid the ring through. "I'll take the twenty euros."

***

"I'm sorry, I've sold it just an hour ago," the shop assistant told Melina with an apologetic grimace.

Melina's shoulders drooped. "Please, tell me that you've got another one."

"No. Sorry. I can check if we can order another one."

"But I need it for tomorrow!"

"How about Chanel Number Five? It's perfect for a mature lady."

"My mother-in-law loves lemons sweets. I need the lemon blossom perfume!"

The shop assistant looked at her as if she was a little crazy.

Melina scoured the narrow streets that led to the city centre, asking in every *profumeria* she passed.

Some shopkeepers tried to persuade her that lemon blossom was out of fashion and that she should buy something else. Others pretended that it didn't exist. Most tried to bully her into buying whatever they wanted to shift. When darkness fell and the shops turned on their glittery lights, Melina was still out on her quest.

The marble floor of the most expensive *profumeria* in Palermo was so shiny that Melina wondered if people could see under her skirt.

Undaunted, she went in and asked for the lemon blossom perfume. The shop assistant's eyes lit up.

"You're very lucky: we were just about to dispo—ahem, discount the last bottle." She went through a back door and emerged with just the thing Melina was looking for. "It's down to fifty per cent of the original price: from forty to twenty euros."

Melina grinned and paid.

***

"What have you got in that bag?" Melina asked Tanino when they were travelling in the lift up to his mother's flat.

Tanino grunted. Women had handbags, but for men it was almost impossible to conceal any object that didn't fit into their pockets!

"Nothing important."

"It looks like a bottle. Is it wine?"

"Limoncello," he lied. Well, almost: it was a lemony alcoholic liquid, after all.

"It's a bit small," she said.

"Are we going to argue about how stingy I am to my mother?"

"No, we aren't."

Melina smiled smugly, which made him a little nervous, even though he knew that his boat was watertight this time.

His mother opened the door with her usual cheer and insisted on bringing out a packet of crisps and a bottle of lemonade for them, even after they refused. When she went to the kitchen to get the glasses, Tanino followed her.

"Mamma, I have a little present for

you."

"Oh, Tanino, you shouldn't have!"

"A hundredth birthday doesn't come every day."

His mum carefully peeled off the wrapping paper. "Oh, Tanino, a lemon blossom perfume! My favourite. You really shouldn't have spent this money on me." She hugged him and stamped a kiss on his cheek.

"Did Melina choose it?"

"No. I did."

"Oh, my boy!" She stamped a kiss on his other cheek and gave him another hug. "Let's not leave Melina alone." She put the perfume down and they picked up the glasses.

As they walked in, they found Melina there with a parcel in her hands and a grin on her face.

"Happy Birthday from Tanino and me," she said, offering the parcel.

His mother shot Tanino a puzzled look. "Again?"

Now it was Melina who looked

puzzled.

His mother made short work of the wrapping paper and finally lifted a bottle out of the scrunched paper. Lemon blossom perfume, exactly the same as Tanino had just given her.

"I'm not sure I'm going to live long enough to use all this lemon blossom perfume," she joked.

***

"Why didn't you tell me that you wanted to buy a present for my mother?" Tanino asked Melina on the way home from the pawn shop.

"And you could have told me why you wanted to save money this month," she replied.

"Yes, I should have. And I'm glad that my mum has given you one of the bottles of perfume. You were going to lose one of your favourite rings for her, poor you." He held her hand and touched the ring, then paused. "I'm intrigued about something. I paid twenty-five euros for that perfume, but the pawn shop only gave you twenty euros. How did you buy it?"

She lifted her chin and grinned.

"I got a discount. Some of us are very careful with money."

4. THE SLEEP DOCTOR

It was on Monday 14th of August that Angelina decided to go to her GP.

Sandwiched as it was between the Sunday holiday and the public holiday of the Assumption of the Virgin Mary, that day was what Italians call a *ponte*—a bridge, a link between two holidays.

In the heat of the Sicilian August, her GP was bound to be off to the seaside with her family, leaving the private surgery in the hands of her substitute: her retired father.

He was the one that Angelina wanted.

Sergio Lombardi had been her GP for donkey's years, but on his seventieth birthday, he had handed the helm of the practice over to his daughter.

As he carried on working only on Fridays, his most devoted patients learned to put up with their aches, coughs and worries from Friday to Friday.

Things became more difficult on Dr Sergio's eightieth birthday, when he stopped his Friday surgery and went down to only covering for his daughter's holidays.

His patients now had to keep their ailments and nerves for weeks, if they didn't want to be seen by his daughter instead.

Claudia Lombardi was a highly qualified doctor—better qualified, in fact, than her father—and a perfectly pleasant woman. But she had a fault.

Instead of trying to get to the bottom of her patients' issues, she immediately referred them to the specialist.

She could go through hundreds of patients in one day, sending them off with a referral letter in their hands. By doing this, she had immensely improved the surgery's efficiency.

But patients like Angelina were not so keen to traipse the city to find specialists whose names—gastroenter-something, ophthal-something else—she couldn't even pronounce.

Once, Angelina went to Dr Claudia because she was worried about some spots that had appeared over her body. She was immediately sent to the dermatologist who told her that she had psoriasis and gave her an ointment. Angelina used the ointment but the spots kept coming back.

So she waited for the week between Christmas and New Year, when Dr Sergio would be holding the fort while his daughter was off skiing with her family, and she managed to be seen by him.

He didn't just check Angelina's spots, but took her blood pressure, her pulse, checked her eyes and had a good look inside her throat.

"These tonsils are rotten! They need to come out! Each time they get infected, they trigger your psoriasis."

Sure enough, after her tonsillectomy, Angelina bade goodbye to her psoriasis.

***

Angelina got to the surgery twenty minutes before the opening time, but she was already the nineteenth patient in the queue.

It seemed all the other fans of Dr Sergio had had the same idea. She resigned herself to waiting patiently. After all, patients are called that for a reason.

This time, Angelina's problem was more difficult than the psoriasis issue. She had already seen Dr Claudia about it and had been prescribed some pills that had made hardly any difference to her complaint and had given her an upset tummy.

"Good morning, Angelina." Dr Sergio rose from his chair and offered his hand when her turn finally arrived. "How are you?"

"I can't sleep at night, Doctor."

***

"You can't sleep at night. Do you mean that you can sleep in the day?"

Dr Sergio's question wasn't sarcastic, but genuine. He had often seen patients complaining that they couldn't sleep at night, only afterwards revealing that they enjoyed long afternoon siestas after large lunches of lasagne and wine.

"I don't know about sleeping in the day. I never let myself have an afternoon nap in case it messes up with my sleep at night."

"Very good."

"It doesn't seem to make any difference, though. Every night I fall asleep like a stone but then I keep waking up every hour or so." Angelina sighed.

Dr Sergio put on his near-vision glasses and pulled down the patient's eyelids to check their colour. Then he checked her throat, her heart and her lungs, like he did with every patient, every time. He'd often found that people didn't know what was troubling them. What they complained about was often not their real problem, so he always checked all the basics anyway.

"When did you start having trouble sleeping?"

It was the height of summer and the temperature at night rarely dipped below the thirties. Anyone would have trouble sleeping in that heat without air-conditioning.

"Since Christmas."

This excluded the heat hypothesis, then.

"Do you share a bed with your husband?"

"Yes."

"You said your trouble started after Christmas, right?"

"Yes."

"Do you have a recent photo of him?"

Angelina looked surprised, but she whipped her mobile phone out of her bag, flicked her finger over the screen, then showed him a photo of a portly man sitting in a restaurant by the sea.

Dr Sergio nodded. His suspicions might be correct.

"Angelina, I want you to take this home." He handed her a tape-recorder. His attempts to keep up with technology had stopped at magnetic tape-recorders. "Put it by your bedside and press record before you go to sleep. Then come back and we'll listen to it together."

***

Angelina was a little surprised by her doctor's request, but she trusted him with her own life—quite literally—so she promptly did as he had asked her.

The next day being again a public holiday, the surgery was open and manned by Dr Sergio.

"The moment of truth," he said, winding back the tape.

Angelina held her breath, even though she was not sure what they were looking for.

As the doctor pressed play, out of the machine came a rustling of sheets followed by silence, occasionally interrupted by a distant police siren or a scooter with a broken exhaust.

Dr Sergio wound the tape forward, stopping at regular intervals to listen.

Around one hour into the recording, as he pressed play again, a formidable sound jolted Angelina against the chair's back rest.

"Goodness me, what's that, Doctor?"

It had sounded like a very large and very wild boar.

"If my prediction is correct, it's your husband, snoring."

They kept listening until, a little later, there was a rustling of sheets and the roaring stopped.

"What happened?"

"The noise woke you, you stirred and that made your husband resurface from his sleep just enough to stop snoring."

The doctor put away the tape and started scribbling on his prescription booklet.

"Here—a prescription for your husband."

Angelina looked at her doctor with surprise.

"It's simple," he went on. "Your husband must have put on weight last Christmas, as people do. The extra weight around his neck has made him start snoring. Here's a diet plan for him."

"Thank you, Doctor."

He scribbled again. "And ear plugs for you."

***

While the diet plan took a little time to work—not least because it encountered some resistance on her husband's part—the ear plugs worked from first application.

As soon as Angelina moulded the blue silicon dough into her ears, a beautiful silence enveloped her. Gone were the police sirens, the scooters with broken exhaust pipes and the wild boar in the bedroom. That night, for the first time in months, Angelina enjoyed an uninterrupted night's sleep.

The following morning, unable to contain her happiness, she spread the news to all her friends and family.

Many of them confessed that they, too, had trouble sleeping and asked for her "sleep doctor's" address.

***

When his daughter had asked him to cover for her three-week holiday in the USA, Sergio had agreed with pleasure. But now that he was in his third week, he felt a little tired.

Patients thronged the waiting-room from early morning till late in the evening. Curiously, many seemed to have sleep problems.

"No coffee after dinner," he told a sleepless patient with coffee-stained teeth.

"Keep your smartphone out of your bedroom," he told a patient who kept checking his phone during the consultation.

"When you are in bed, let your wife talk to you to her heart's content," he advised.

"Exercise more," he instructed a patient who dropped her body heavily on to the chair.

As more and more people flocked to him with their sleep trouble and were cured, Dr Sergio's reputation was consolidated.

On the last day of the last week, Sergio was weary. The flow of patients had become a little punishing. Working one day a week, on a Friday, had suited him well in the past, but working every day was a little too much for a man his age.

After his twentieth patient, he decided to take an informal little break. He folded his arms on his desk, laid his head on them and, gazing at the tree out of the window, he let his eyelids droop just a little...

***

Luca had been told by his aunt Angelina about the wonderful Dr Sergio. He confessed he was a little doubtful about a specialist doctor called a "sleep doctor".

Specialists usually had difficult names. Still, given that today was the man's last day covering for his daughter, Luca decided he could do worse than give him a try.

When the receptionist called his name, Luca sprang to his feet and walked down the corridor, hoping that the sleep doctor knew his stuff.

He knocked gently on the door and, without waiting for an answer, opened it and walked in.

As soon as he saw the doctor, Luca was much relieved. The man did know his stuff. With his head resting on his arms and a smile on his lips, the doctor was fast asleep.

5. TANINO'S CHAIR

The weather had already turned sticky in the Sicilian capital of Palermo. A hot and bothered Melina pushed the broom around her husband's armchair and darted it a fiery scowl.

She hated this chair with all her heart. The ancient foam had turned brittle and was crumbling away. No sooner had she swept the patches of orange dust underneath the chair than new ones showered down. The worn and tattered upholstery constantly reminded her that fifty years had passed since she and Tanino were newly married, which was when the chair had moved in with them.

And that the hours Tanino spent on it

snoozing, watching TV, doing his crosswords, were times when her husband could have paid attention to her instead. Or helped in the house.

But if Melina mentioned the orange foam dust, Tanino dismissed it as ant droppings. If she pointed out the torn upholstery, he patched it up with sticky tape. If she questioned him about the missing front feet, he assured her that it was easier to get up from a chair that tilted forward. As much as Melina hated that chair, Tanino loved it. Not for nothing, in Italian, 'armchair' was a feminine noun. So, all she could do was push the chair closer to the door, but never out of the room.

She energetically swept the last foam crumbs, put away dustpan and broom and set off to the church for the Sacred Heart novena. There she prayed that, if she was ever foolish enough to set her husband an ultimatum and choose between keeping her or the chair, he would choose her.

"We're thinking of starting a mother-and-baby group in the parish," Father Pino announced at the end of the novena. "It will be a space for mothers to meet and socialise while their children play. But we need volunteers to help run it and donations of toys, children's books, crockery and chairs."

Chairs? Melina's heart somersaulted. The parish needed Tanino's chair! If this wasn't God answering her prayer!

Her feet skimmed the marble tiles as she rushed from her pew to the sacristy, where she found Father Pino still wriggling out of his vestments. "I've got a lovely armchair that I'm happy to donate, Father!" she announced.

"Actually, I was thinking of chairs, not armchairs."

"But you must have at least one armchair, for breastfeeding mothers." Melina planted herself between Father Pino and the door.

"Well, that shows that I don't know anything about these things. Thanks,

Melina. I'll send someone to collect it this week."

"No, they must come now," she said urgently.

If they came to collect the chair when Tanino was home, he would say no. Right now, Tanino was at the café with his friends and he wouldn't return home until lunchtime.

"OK, Melina. I'll send Salvatore over with you now."

When Salvatore saw the chair, his expression suggested that he didn't like it any more than Melina did.

"What's all that orange stuff on the floor?" He pointed to the crumbled foam.

"Ant droppings," Melina replied.

She watched from her balcony with satisfaction as the young man strapped the chair to his three-wheeled Piaggio Ape and drove off.

Mission accomplished. Now she needed to buy Tanino a replacement. She would buy it with the money from

Aunt Rosa's inheritance. It would be her present to Tanino.

She put her saving account's chequebook in her handbag and went to the furniture shop down the road.

"You can choose any combination of features: model, size, fabric…anything," the shopkeeper told her, pushing a thick catalogue in front of her.

Melina hadn't realised there could be so much choice: soft chairs, hard chairs, tilting and tipping chairs that could make you seasick and chairs that massaged you.

It took her a few hours to select every detail to make sure that Tanino would not miss his old chair. Finally, it was all agreed and paid.

"Great. I'll call you around the first week of September to let you know when your chair will be delivered," the shopkeeper said.

"September?" It was more than two months away. Where would Tanino sit till then?

The shopkeeper shrugged. "Chairs like this are custom-made and in August all the factories are shut for the summer holidays. You won't get your dream chair from us or any other shop unless you're prepared to wait."

***

It was almost one o'clock and Tanino was looking forward to one of Melina's delicious lunches. Would it be pasta, rice or pizza?

The lift doors opened but no delicious smells wafted into his nostrils.

He stuck the keys into the lock of his flat and opened the door. Immediately a void stared at him. Something was missing from the sitting-room but he wasn't sure what.

"Hello!"

He walked into the kitchen to face another absence: where was his wife? Tanino checked his watch, then the clock ticking on the wall. It was definitely one o'clock, but there was no lunch on the stove and no Melina.

Should he call the police?

He heard keys turning in the lock and the creaking of the front door. Melina! He scuttled to the hall.

"Melina, my sparrow, is everything OK?"

"Yes," she said, but her crinkled forehead told the contrary.

"What's the matter?"

His gaze snagged on something peeking out of her handbag. A furniture catalogue. The penny dropped.

"My chair! Where's my chair?"

"I'm really sorry, Tanino."

"What have you done with my chair?" He felt his pulse in his neck.

"The parish has taken it, but I've bought you a new one," she replied, avoiding his gaze.

"Taken it? You must have given it to them. Why would you give away my chair?"

"They needed it for the mother and toddler group."

"Why didn't you buy them a new

chair?" He was hopping from one foot to the other. "You can't give away things that don't belong to you!"

"We've always said that everything that's mine is yours and everything that's yours is mine…" She nervously twisted the hem of her shirt.

"But not my chair!" Tanino held his head in his hands and shook it left to right. "May the Lord forgive you, because I can't!" he yelled.

He stormed into the sitting-room, where he plonked himself on the only remaining armchair—Melina's—and stared at the empty space.

Fittingly, Melina cooked pasta all'arrabbiata (angry pasta). They ate in silence.

Every now and then, Melina glanced at Tanino's face to gauge the extent of the damage she had caused. Bad. And yet it had seemed such a good idea! It was such a pity that the new chair wasn't to be ready for two months.

She had imagined Tanino coming

home to find an all-singing, all-dancing, brand-new tilting chair. He wouldn't have been anywhere near as angry. In fact, he should have been delighted. She hated it when Tanino was angry with her, and even more when he had good reason.

When his expression gradually shifted from bewilderment to sorrowful resignation, she felt thoroughly guilty. "Please, forgive me. I didn't mean it to happen like this. You should have found a new chair waiting when you got home."

All she got out of him was a groan. When he finished his lunch, he plodded into the sitting-room and sat on Melina's chair again without bothering to remove her magazine from the seat.

A prick of indignation pinched her, but she thought better than to raise a complaint and started on the washing-up instead.

For the rest of that afternoon, Tanino dozed on and off, did his crosswords and watched TV. All on Melina's chair. He only got up to use the bathroom but returned immediately after.

The same happened the following day, and the one after that. Melina had been dethroned. She resigned herself to sitting on the uncomfortable sofa and knitting in the light of the window.

***

Tanino hadn't meant it as a revenge or compensation. He had sat in Melina's chair only because she was busy washing up, and he had expected to have to give it up when she had finished. But she never claimed her chair back. So he stayed there all afternoon and until suppertime, just to see how long he could get away with it.

Not a protest escaped her lips that day, or the next, or the one after, even though he made a point of spending all the time he was at home sitting on her chair. It seemed she was aware that she didn't have a leg to stand on—or, in this case, a chair to sit on.

For a few days he had a bit of fun. But after a while, he got tired of it. He guessed that Melina had probably learned her lesson by now and, in any case, he couldn't bear watching her all crumpled on the rock-hard sofa, trying to read her magazine with a hunched back. He did have a heart!

One morning, he got up from her chair and sat on the sofa next to her. She squinted at him over her reading glasses. He threaded an arm around her shoulders.

"Thank you for lending me your chair. You can have it back. I'm going out."

He picked up his crosswords, glasses and Biro, and left.

***

Yes, she was glad to sit on her chair again, but what had really made Melina happy were Tanino's words and his lovely smile. Had he forgiven her? And where had he gone?

At one o'clock the front door opened

and Tanino called from the hall. "I'm home!"

She scuttled to him. "Thank goodness! Where have you been?"

"I went to the parish hall. I wanted to…check on my chair," he said coyly. "Guess what? They've repaired it and reupholstered it! I recognised it only from the shape. The hall was empty so I sat on my chair and started doing my crossword.

"Suddenly there were children's voices in the corridor and, a moment later, lots of mothers and toddlers poured in. They looked a little surprised when they saw me, but when I asked them if they wanted me to leave, they said, 'You can stay, so long as you read a story to the children, because you're sitting on the storytelling chair.' 'Sure,' I said. 'I don't even need to read a story. I can tell them off the top of my head.'

"So I did, starting with the three little pigs, who didn't just build their homes but their chairs, too, and ending with

Pinocchio, who lied to the Blue Fairy and told her that people had taken his schoolbooks, not that he had given them away." Tanino gave Melina a meaningful look and she felt her cheeks flush.

Then he stepped closer and wrapped her in his arms. "Even Pinocchio was forgiven in the end." He kissed her.

"Ah, I almost forgot! They've asked me to go again tomorrow and to bring along someone who can make good coffee. I told them that nobody makes better coffee than you. Would you like to come with me?"

"Very much," she said, and kissed him.

The End.

Other books by Stefania Hartley:

To Be Loved

Amanda's name means "to be loved" and she's taken it as her duty to make herself lovable, but it's hard work. Has Tanino really abandoned Melina to freeze at home? Mark hasn't seen Nora for thirty years and, since then, he's lost a leg and all his hair. If he wasn't enough for her then, how can he be now? What happens if the dating app's algorithms go haywire?

Drive Me Crazy:

"Cohabitation is tribulation" goes an Italian saying, and after more than fifty years of married life, Tanino and Melina know a thing or two about the challenges of living together.

A Slip of the Tongue:

Will Melina regret faking to be sick to avoid her chores? Can Don Pericle organise a wedding for a groom who doesn't know? Who has stolen the marble pisces from the cathedral's floor?

Fresh from the Sea:

Will Gnà Peppina give her customers what they need, even if it's more than food? What pleasures can a man indulge in after his wife has put him on a draconian diet? Who will be able to cook dinner for the family with five euros?

Confetti and Lemon Blossom:
For Don Pericle, wedding organising is a calling, not just a career. Deep in the Sicilian countryside, between rose gardens and trellised balconies, up marble staircases and across damasked ballrooms, these charming stories unfold: stories of star-crossed love, of comedic misunderstandings and of deep friendships, of love triumphing in the face of adversity.

Stars Are Silver:
Is it too late for Melina to learn to drive? Is Don Pericle's vow never to fall in love again still valid after fifty years? Will a falling piano squash Filomena or just shake up her heart? Why does the mother of the bride ask Don Pericle to cancel the wedding?

A Season of Goodwill:
How far should Viviana's family go to avoid being thirteen at the table? Should Melina and Tanino attend a New Year's party

hosted by Melina's old flame? Why do Don Pericle's clients want a Christmas wedding at all costs?

Tales from the Parish:
Father Okoli dreams of owning a flock of hens and studying for a PhD, when his bishop saddles him with yet another parish to look after.

But as Father moves to Moreton-on-the-Edge, a farming village in the English Cotswolds, he's plugged into a community of warm-hearted characters, from the motherly parish secretary to her septuagenarian neighbour who's become a cycling champion, and from teenagers requiring driving lessons to atheist publicans who believe in miracles.

As the community pulls together to reopen the village's Electric Picture House, dreams are fulfilled, teen love blossoms and Father Okoli feels that Moreton-on-the-Edge is now home.

Welcome to Quayside
Forty-year-old Tanya Baker dreams of starting a new life and making friends when she moves to a block of flats by the River Thames with her thirteen-year-old daughter, Hattie. But as Tanya and Hattie knock on

neighbours' doors in search of a tin opener, it's clear that the residents of Number One Quayside like to keep to themselves.

Everyone, that is, except their next-door neighbours, Italian chef Giacomo Dalamo, and his thirteen-year-old daughter, Frankie.

Between a delicious dish of lasagne (Giacomo's) and a burnt salad (Tanya's), they hatch a plan to set a library of things in their building, so that residents can borrow rarely-used items, from DIY tools to sports equipment and party supplies. As all the residents at Quayside pull together to make the library happen, dreams are fulfilled, a community is born and love blossoms again.

The Italian Fake Date:
When Alice Baker discovers that she's been adopted, she knows she won't have peace until she's found her Italian birth mother. But all she has is a letter written twenty-five years ago and an old address.

Jaded about love and unable to forgive his ex-fiancée and his brother, Paolo Rondino is struggling to find inspiration for a sculpture that will make or break his career. Hoping that a trip home will help him find his muse again, he decides to return to Italy, even if this means confronting the two people who betrayed him.

Alice and Paolo strike a deal: he will help her find her birth mother and she will pretend to be his girlfriend to please his mother. It looks like the perfect exchange, until real feelings start to grow…

Sweet Competition for Camillo's Café:
Camillo runs a popular café on Altavicia's main square. Giada runs an equally popular café across the square. They have both entered Altavicia's Best Café competition. Scarred by his father's death, Camillo's greatest wish is to escape the Calabrian seaside village and return to his beloved London, where his family was last together and happy. Abandoned by her parents, Giada's greatest wish is to earn her nonna's love. The competition trophy is the ticket to both their dreams, but only one can win.

As Camillo discovers that happiness doesn't come from a location and Giada that love isn't earned, can enemies become friends, and maybe more?

ABOUT THE AUTHOR

Stefania was born in Sicily and immediately started growing, but not very much. She left her sunny island after falling head over heels in love with an Englishman, and now she lives in the UK with her husband and their three children.

Having finally learnt English, she's enjoying it so much that she now writes novels and short stories which have been longlisted, shortlisted, commended, and won prizes.

If you have enjoyed these stories, please consider leaving a review.

If you want to hear when she's releasing a new book, sign up for her newsletter: www.stefaniahartley.com/subscribe

You'll also receive an exclusive short story.

Printed in Great Britain
by Amazon